25TH ANNIVERSARY EDITION

THE REATION

JAMES WELDON JOHNSON

illustrated by

JAMES E. RANSOME

Holiday House  New York

ILLUSTRATOR'S NOTE

James Weldon Johnson's poetic sermons in God's Trombones: Seven Negro
Sermons in Verse *were influenced by the folk sayings and Southern imagery
of nineteenth-century African-American plantation preachers. I have tried to
remain faithful to the spirit of Mr. Johnson's text by interspersing creation scenes
with images of a Southern country storyteller.*

James E. Ransome

January 15, 1993

Illustrations copyright © 1994 by James E. Ransome
Biographical essay © 2018 by M. Couch
All Rights Reserved
Design by Semadar Megged
HOLIDAY HOUSE is registered in the U.S. Patent and Trademark Office.
Printed and Bound in June 2018 at Tien Wah Press, Johor Bahru, Johor, Malaysia.
www.holidayhouse.com
1 3 5 7 9 10 8 6 4 2

The Library of Congress has cataloged the prior edition as follows.
Library of Congress Cataloging-in-Publication Data
The Creation / by James Weldon Johnson ; illustrated by James Ransome. — 1st ed. p. cm.
Summary: A poem based on the story of creation from the first book of the Bible.
ISBN 0-8234-1069-2
1. Creation—Juvenile poetry. 2. Children's poetry, American.
[1. Creation—Poetry. 2—American poetry—Afro American authors.
3. Bible stories—O.T.] I. Ransome, James. II. Johnson, James Weldon, 1871–1938. Creation.
PS3519.O2625C73   1994 93–3207   CIP   AC
811'.52—dc20

ISBN 978-0-8234-4025-2 (hardcover)

To African-American artists who have succeeded with dignity and pride:

Romare Bearden

William H. Johnson

Tom Feelings

Ernest Crichlow

Jerry Pinkney

Henry O. Tanner

Jacob Lawrence

E. Simms Campbell

Robert Freeman

to name only a few . . . all who have touched my life.

JAMES E. RANSOME

ND God stepped out on space,—
And He looked around and said,
"I'm lonely—
I'll make me a world."

And far as the eye of God could see
Darkness covered everything,
Blacker than a hundred midnights
Down in a cypress swamp.

Then God smiled,
And the light broke,
And the darkness rolled up on one side,
And the light stood shining on the other,
And God said, *"That's good!"*

THEN God reached out and took the
light in His hands,

And God rolled the light around in His hands

Until He made the sun;

And He set that sun a-blazing in the heavens.

And the light that was left from making the sun

God gathered up in a shining ball

And flung against the darkness,

Spangling the night with the moon and stars.

Then down between

The darkness and the light

He hurled the world;

And God said, "*That's good!*"

THEN God Himself stepped down—
And the sun was on His right hand,
And the moon was on His left;
The stars were clustered about His head,
And the earth was under His feet.
And God walked, and where He trod
His footsteps hollowed the valleys out
And bulged the mountains up.

HEN He stopped and looked and saw

That the earth was hot and barren.

So God stepped over to the edge of the world

And He spat out the seven seas;

He batted His eyes, and the lightnings flashed;

He clapped His hands, and the thunders rolled;

And the waters above the earth came down,

The cooling waters came down.

HEN the green grass sprouted,

And the little red flowers blossomed,

The pine-tree pointed his finger to the sky,

And the oak spread out his arms;

The lakes cuddled down in the hollows of the ground,

And the rivers ran down to the sea;

And God smiled again,

And the rainbow appeared,

And curled itself around His shoulder.

HEN God raised His arm and
He waved His hand
Over the sea and over the land,
And He said, *"Bring forth! Bring forth!"*
And quicker than God could drop His hand,
Fishes and fowls
And beasts and birds
Swam the rivers and the seas,
Roamed the forests and the woods,
And split the air with their wings,
And God said, *"That's good!"*

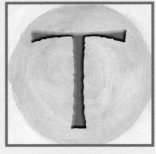

THEN God walked around,
And God looked around
On all that He had made.
He looked at His sun,
And He looked at His moon,
And He looked at His little stars;
He looked on His world
With all its living things,
And God said, "I'm lonely still."

Then God sat down
On the side of a hill where He could think;
By a deep, wide river He sat down;
With His head in His hands,
God thought and thought,
Till He thought, "I'll make me a man!"

P from the bed of the river

God scooped the clay;

And by the bank of the river

He kneeled Him down;

And there the great God Almighty

Who lit the sun and fixed it in the sky,

Who flung the stars to the most far corner of the night,

Who rounded the earth in the middle of His hand—

This Great God,

Like a mammy bending over her baby,

Kneeled down in the dust

Toiling over a lump of clay

Till He shaped it in His own image;

THEN into it He blew the breath of life,
And man became a living soul.

WHO WAS JAMES WELDON JOHNSON?

JAMES WELDON JOHNSON was a leading light of the Harlem Renaissance and a man of extraordinary talents. Born in Jacksonville, Florida, in 1871 to middle-class parents—his mother was an English teacher and his father head of dining staff at the St. James Hotel—he was a gifted child and an exceptional student. In 1891 he was accepted by a historically Black college in Atlanta, Clark Atlanta University, where he spent a formative summer teaching Black children in the backwoods of Georgia and graduated valedictorian in 1894.

He became a teacher at Jacksonville's Stanton School, a grammar school for Black children, and in 1895 he founded The Daily American, an afternoon paper that focused on pressing Black issues. In 1897 he was one of the first Black lawyers admitted to the Florida Bar, and he ran a successful law practice concurrent with his new duties as principal of the Stanton School. He added the ninth and tenth grades to Stanton, making it the first public Black high school in Florida, and in 1901 he was elected president of the Florida State Teachers Association.

That same year, Johnson and his talented brother, John Rosamond, a composer who had graduated from the New England Conservatory of Music in 1897, left the South for New York City as part of the Great Migration. There they joined the Black social and cultural milieu that preceded the Harlem Renaissance, becoming successful musical writers for Broadway and producing more than two hundred songs, including "The Old Flag Never Touched the Ground," "Didn't He Ramble," and "Tell Me, Dusky Maiden." It was during this period that Johnson penned the famous anthem "Lift Ev'ry Voice and Sing," which became the official song of the NAACP.

At the same time, Johnson studied creative writing at Columbia University at the graduate level and became very active in Republican politics. He was the treasurer of the New York Colored Republicans Club and wrote two songs for Theodore Roosevelt's presidential campaign. He also accepted membership in the Society of International Law.

In 1906, President Roosevelt appointed Johnson as a diplomat, and he served as U.S. consul in Venezuela and then Nicaragua through 1913. In 1910, he married Grace Nail, a Black feminist, activist, and socialite who founded the NAACP Junior League, and in 1912 he published The Autobiography of an Ex-Colored Man, his only novel and one of his greatest works.

Returning to New York City in 1913, he busied himself with the arts, becoming a contributing editor to the distinguished Black newspaper New York Age and translating Fernando Periquet's grand opera Goyescas from the Spanish. It was performed by the Metropolitan Opera in 1915.

In 1916, his friend W. E. B. DuBois urged him to accept an NAACP post, and he became the organization's field secretary, promoted to executive secretary in 1920. Johnson helped found new NAACP chapters all across the South, dramatically increasing membership, and in 1917 he led a silent march of 10,000 people down Fifth Avenue to protest federal inaction on lynching.

In 1922, he edited the landmark anthology The Book of American Negro Poetry, followed in 1925 by another anthology, The Book of American Negro Spirituals, and then The Second Book of American Negro Spirituals in 1926, classic collections of Black poetry, verse, and voice. Inspired, he wrote God's Trombones: Seven Negro Sermons in Verse, which was published in 1927. Regarded as his best work, this is the poetry book in which "The Creation" first appeared. Johnson's interest in and celebration of the rural Black experience and all varieties of Black vernacular was lifelong.

In 1930, he resigned from the NAACP to become chair of creative writing at Fisk University, a historically Black school in Nashville, Tennessee, and in 1934 he became the first African American professor at New York University, where he lectured on literature. Black Manhattan, his study of Black contributions to the arts in New York City, was published in 1930, followed by his autobiography, Along This Way (1933); his rumination on civil rights, Negro Americans, What Now? (1934); and Saint Peter Relates an Incident: Selected Poems (1934), his last poetry collection.

While on vacation in Maine in 1938, he died tragically in an automobile accident. More than two thousand people attended his Harlem funeral.